I Want My Dinner

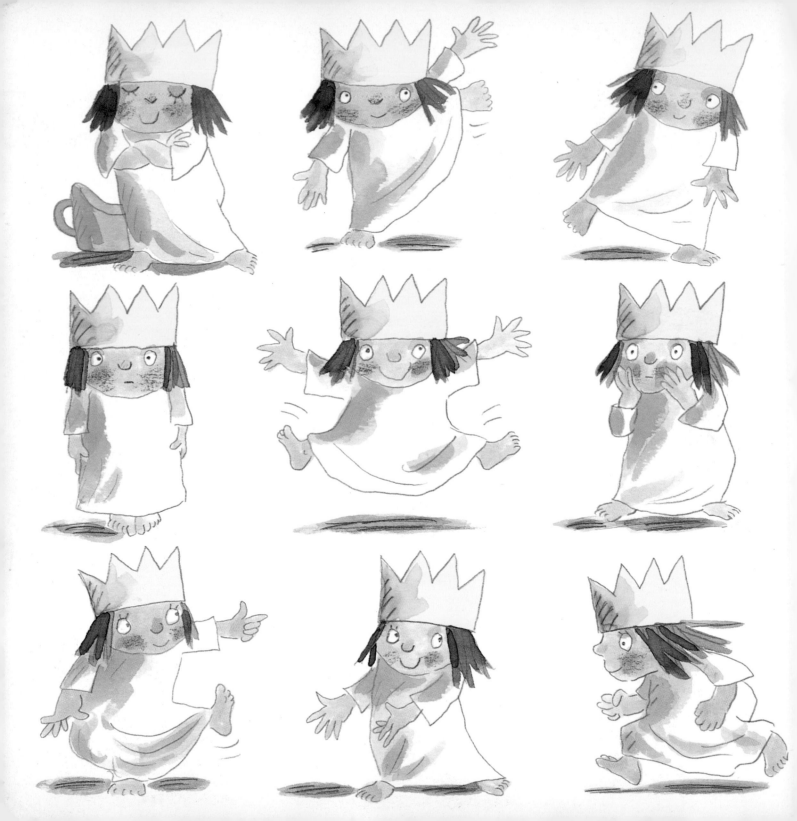

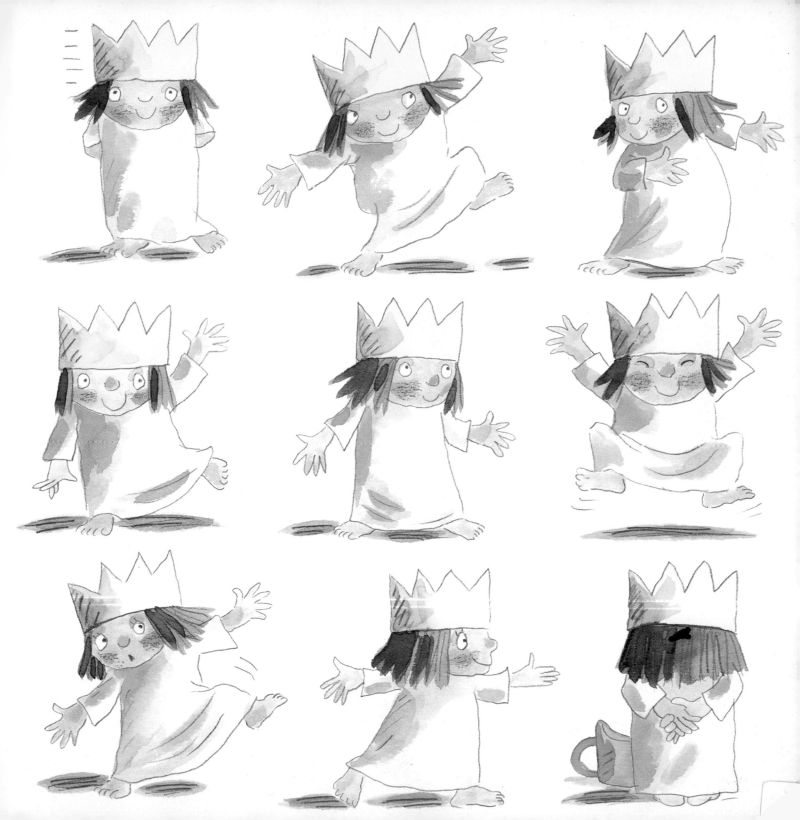

First published in Great Britain by Andersen Press Ltd in 1995.
First published in Picture Lions in 1996.
10 9 8 7 6 5 4 3 2 1
Picture Lions is an imprint of the Children's Division,
part of HarperCollins Publishers Ltd,
77-85 Fulham Palace Road, Hammersmith,
London, W6 8JB.
Copyright © Tony Ross 1995
The author/illustrator asserts the moral right to be
identified as the author/illustrator of this work.
ISBN: 0 00 664356 6
Printed and bound in Hong Kong

I Want My Dinner

Tony Ross

PictureLions

An Imprint of HarperCollinsPublishers

"I WANT MY DINNER!"

"Say PLEASE," said the Queen.

"I want my dinner . . . please."

"Mmmmm, lovely."

"I want my potty."

"Say PLEASE," said the General.

"I want my potty, PLEASE."

"Mmmmm, lovely."

"I want my Teddy . . .

. . . PLEASE," said the Princess.

"Mmmmm."

"We want to go for a walk . . . PLEASE."

"Mmmmm."

"Mmmmm . . . that looks good."

"HEY!" said the Beastie.

"That's MY dinner."

"I want my dinner!"

"Say PLEASE," said the Princess.

"I want my dinner, PLEASE."

"Mmmmm."

"HEY!" said the Princess.

"Say THANK YOU."

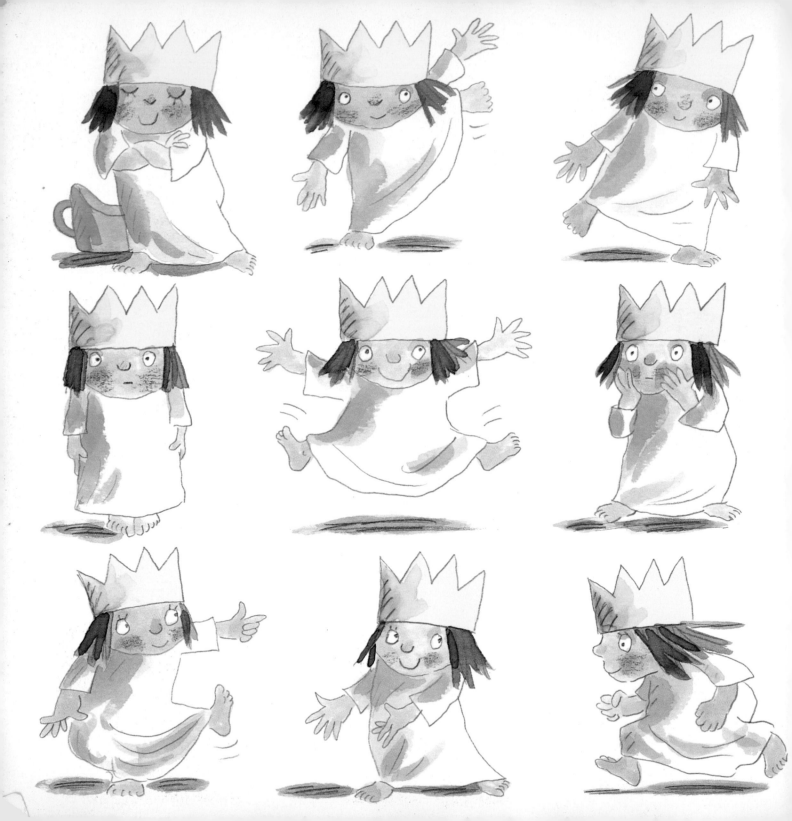

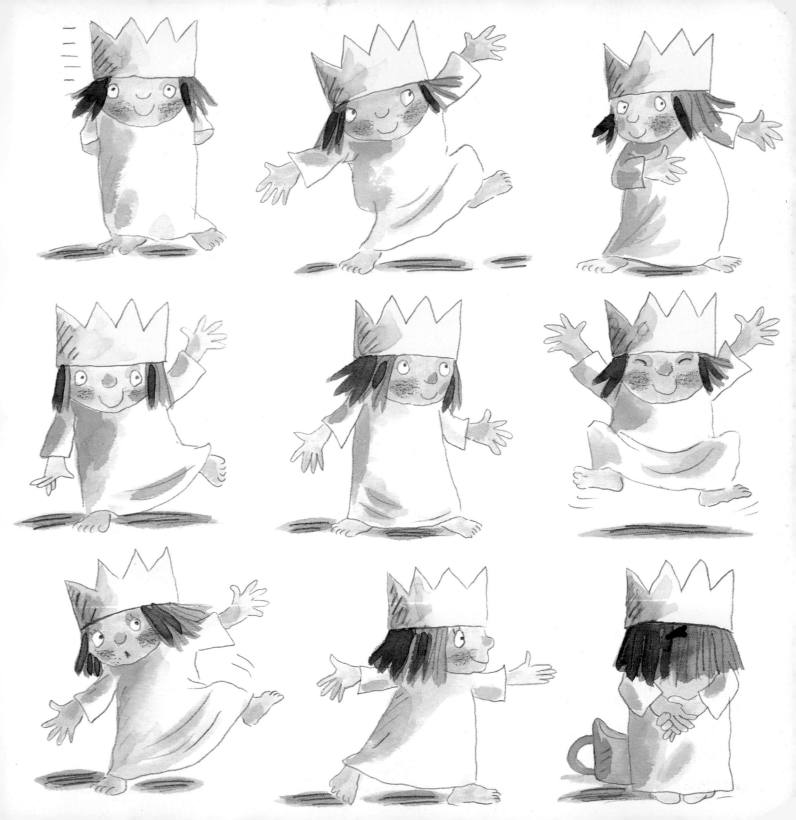

Collins
Picture Lions

Have you read all these stories by Tony Ross?

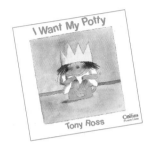 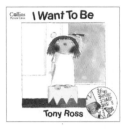 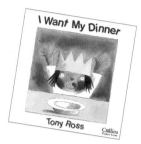

 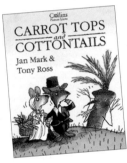  

 Listen out for these stories on tape:

I WANT MY POTTY • I WANT TO BE • I WANT MY DINNER • STONE SOUP • RECKLESS RUBY